STORIES OF
HAPPY LOVERS
— *and* —
UNHAPPY WIVES

BY DAVINA FERREIRA

davina@alegriamagazine.com

ISBN: 978-1-7361496-5-2
Published by Alegria publishing

Illustration and cover by Tania Peregrino
Book layout by Sirenas Creative

I call her Wild Woman, for those very words, wild and woman, create llamar o tocar a la puerta, the fairy-tale knock at the door of the deep feminine psyche. Llamar o tocar a la puerta means literally to play upon the instrument of the name in order to open a door. It means using words that summon up the opening of a passageway. No matter by which culture a woman is influenced, she understands the words wild and woman, intuitively.

-Clarissa Pinkola Estés

Preface

I am passionate about discovering why we, as women, devote ourselves to loving others more than we love ourselves. Why do we focus on everyone else's needs and neglect our own? I know we can sense the life that dwells within us like an ocean filled with possibility. I know we can reach that brilliant shore of our unlived dreams.

I am feeling more awake today than at any point during the past decade of my life. I write this after being transformed — living through a catharsis that only loss and heartbreak could set in motion. Today, I find myself on the verge of understanding the magnitude of my soul's path. Today, love is — and I believe will always continue to be — the vena cava of my spiritual and artistic search. Love is the artery that allows for an uninterrupted flow of creativity, a channel that connects my entire body of work to the whole of my being.

Now, more than ever, I recognize myself in the lives of other women — women who, just like me, can choose not only whom to love but how to live. This, of course, is if one is lucky enough to live in a part of the world where our marriages are not forced upon us, and where being sold into the sex trade isn't commonplace. If we are so fortunate to have the freedom to choose our path, we must — or we risk leaving our treasured dreams of self-realization behind, buried inside the trunks of our unfulfilled desires.

To be a Happy Lover is to be empowered and not merely a victim of love's twisted fate. It's my way of honoring my current state of being — giving it a name and embracing its meaning.

To be a Happy Lover is to be active, not passive. This name is given to a group of women who not only give to others but who, even more importantly, make a point of being kind and generous by giving to themselves.

I once lost someone I loved dearly and, while painful, it also forced me to look at my relationship with myself. I had a breakthrough which, as the word suggests, involves a rupture — it's an awakening born from pain. I broke away from patterns that kept me going in circles, and which led me to confuse being numb with being comfortable.

I also know what makes an Unhappy Wife (since I have also been there myself) and I spoke to many of them when drawing inspiration for these stories. Unhappy Wives gather to vent and find relief in the healing powers of storytelling and female camaraderie. For it seems that domesticated love has its own price, its light and its shadow. And yet, there are also Happy Wives (I have also been one), who recognize the beautiful power that comes from being in a kind, supportive and lasting partnership, one that can have a tremendous impact on our growth.

Until now, I never understood that I had the key to open any door I wanted. I never understood how powerful being a Happy Lover could be when the love was directed by me, toward me, in harmony with my creativity and spirituality.

This is how the painter is moved to grab her brush and begin her creation, after feeling so lost and lackluster — inventing shapes so unimaginable that her inner Dalí starts to smile again. This is how so many female creators will come to design the best sculptures in the gallery of their dreams; how the poet will write in the style of her lyric soul; how the frustrated actress will once again step onto the stage. Every woman will awaken to her unexplored parallel life of inner brilliance, perhaps deeply buried, but still living as a desert flower.

They will feel that it is possible to be happy once again.

Returning to a life of adventures, the Happy Lover will find a world that arouses new inspiration. She will summon her strengths, new powers that allow her to explode in the embrace of a forgotten pleasure. She will clearly see how her happiness does not spring from a partner, be they male or female, nor is it tied to a need. Rather, her happiness comes from a union within herself, from her parallel world of pleasure, and from her artistic and spiritual expansion. She will surprise herself as she discovers new possibilities — boundaries that seem to know no bounds. And, as she redefines failure and frustration when it comes to love, she will open the doors to new dimensions so expansive that her whole being can fill as much space as it desires.

Before I ever believed myself to be a Happy Lover, I lived an illusion. I loved the feeling of being in love; it was the best drug. But, like all drugs, if not controlled, it had the potential to destroy. I crossed that line on more than one occasion. I turned myself over to love only to release its power, a power that will possess and consume everything in its clutches. Eros and Thanatos. Death and life. How easy it is to go from heaven to hell.

As for how I created these stories — or who these Happy Lovers might be — that must be left to your imagination. I have been lucky enough to share quality time with hundreds of women from all walks of life. While no two stories are the same, any of these women could be any of us — a Happy Lover, an Unhappy Wife, or someone in between. And all of these women can teach all of us what it means to be free.

BY DAVINA FERREIRA

⬡ @davifalegria
✉ davina@alegriamagazine.com

Table Of Contents

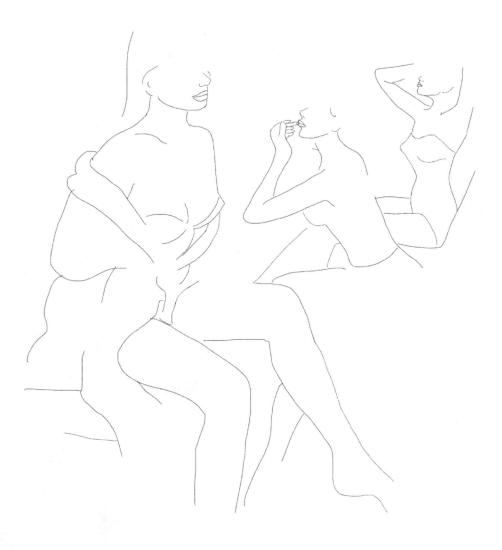

"A woman who owns her freedom and her aura, terrifies.
Sweetness and death in one single gaze."

Awakening

Was I asleep?

*Sleepwalking with my dreams
under my sleeve,*

*Dishes piled up
&
Cracked hands,
remembering their softness.*

*What would it take
For me
To truly awaken?*

I was divorced at forty. Caring for my three children was my only reason for getting up in the morning. If it weren't for them, I wouldn't be here after so much pain.

I couldn't let my children into my crumbling world. During the short showers I took, the water hit my face and ran down my cheeks with my tears. Late at night I turned to my pillow to absorb those agonizing sounds I needed to stay behind closed doors. There had been no time for recovery. During the day, my children gave me the direction and purpose I knew I needed to survive. Baby steps, before I could even think of how I might learn to thrive.

That summer morning was different. The sunlight hit my bathroom mirror in a certain way; at a certain angle perhaps, I'll never be sure. But there I stood, again, just like any other day, but standing in those rays of sun, I started to notice the inevitable passage of time in my face and my body. I caught a glimpse of someone far away but familiar. That's when I felt the shift. There was still so much inside of me, so much more living to do and to experience. I knew I had to face my fears, to go out into the world, and to become *me* again.

I had finally admitted that my little ones weren't so little anymore, and decided I could trust them with a babysitter. But could I trust myself to make it through a few hours away from home? My girlfriends never gave up on me, but they always gave me space, inviting me to go out with them but never insisting. This time, when the invite came, I decided to escape for a summer night. I would finally step out with my girlfriends again, out into the City of Angels, where the scent of bougainvillea permeated the air, and the sweetness of an evening breeze could wrap around my shoulders — lightly blowing on my skin in ways that I had not felt in over a decade.

I pulled out the only little black dress I still had hanging in my closet from my pre-pregnancy days. To my surprise, it still fit. This alone gave me a much-needed boost. The dress hugged my curves as if it wanted to embrace me, holding me up and saying: *you can do this*. It brought back a long-forgotten desire to curl my long hair and put on my black stiletto heels. I could feel a jolt of excitement running through me as I quenched my 'mom guilt' with a shot of tequila, before opening my front door and setting out on my first girls' night out in more than a decade.

> *It is me.*
> *A new me I am ready to meet.*
> *A wiser woman and, why not, maybe a more seasoned lover?*

When I made it to the restaurant and my girlfriends saw me, their reactions could not have been more perfect:
"Gurlllllll, you look hoooottt!"
They gave me the extra boost of confidence I needed.

I couldn't help but notice two younger guys, maybe in their early thirties, following me with their eyes as I made my way to the bar.

Thank God for tequila, I thought to myself.

I kept walking, knowing that before I reached the bar, I would be passing those men. I looked straight ahead, never making eye contact — but I did weave ever so slightly to the right which brought me closer to them. As I passed, I could feel them catch that scent of fresh prey. For me, it was more than a smell. I realized it was also a taste — one I had not had near my lips or nose in a long while.

The most outgoing of the two started the small talk:
"You look beautiful tonight, where are you from?"
"I grew up on the East Coast, but my parents are from El Salvador," I said.
"Nice… Latina!"
"Yes, that's right," I replied, "and very proud of it."
"Well, let me introduce you to my friend, Ahmad. He is here visiting from Saudi."
I smiled and took the second man's hand. "Nice to meet you, Ahmad. My name is Kim."
"Nice to meet you too, Kim," he said.

I looked away. Time for my next tequila shot — and I really needed it now; in that short exchange, Ahmad had given me a look that threw me off balance. The intrigue was so strong. He had that beautiful Middle Eastern mystery, a cultural heritage that always fascinated me. Just one glimpse into his eyes and I was reliving dreams I thought I would never have again. My faded fantasies were reappearing right in front of me.

Given my responsibilities as a mother, I had never considered traveling to the Middle East. My children always came first, and I was content with that. I knew motherhood came with a high price, but I was prepared to make those sacrifices. I had put so many of my desires and pleasures on hold.

Did I want to travel to faraway lands and experience the world?

Absolutely.

Ahmad, with his beautiful green eyes, had lit a fire in me, sparking dormant dreams. And I had many more.

I yearned to meet a young man like Ahmad and make crazy, wild love, without attachment or reservation, letting myself come as many times as possible without any cares about my weight or stretch marks or cellulite. I wanted to give this pleasure to myself in all its glory, not in service to anyone but myself.

That night, Ahmad seemed like the ideal candidate, and after my third tequila shot, I felt ready. I walked back to join my girlfriends, who seemed to be enjoying watching me wake up. They could see my smile and they knew, better than anyone, how desperately I needed this evening. Once I told them about Ahmad and his friends, sharing details about his intense looks, they were more than determined to make sure things did not stop there.

The girls were all on a mission, but Kate and Liz, the most social of the group, made sure the boys knew they were welcome to hang with us — and that we were ready to party. They had made their way to the bar, spoken with Ahmad and his friends, and invited them back to our table.

As he approached, there was a second glance. Then, a third. And soon he was right there, at our table, standing so close to me I thought I could hear his heart beating. Or was it mine? A few hours of endless conversation and flirtation took place between us while the world around us disappeared…

I was under his spell, and perhaps I had cast one over him as well, because time stopped for both Ahmad and me. He did not tell me much about his life; I told him far too much about mine. But, by doing so, I felt freer than I had in a decade. I was not about to become preoccupied with more self-conscious distraction. I did not feel like explaining or apologizing. I simply wanted to own my story, my whole story, as an adult woman.

Ahmad listened and the more he listened the more his green eyes penetrated me. Every inch of my body trembled. He had ignited a passion buried within me — a passion that had grown dull after giving myself a thousand and one lonely orgasms using fantasies that had lost their power over time.

He touched every part of me with his eyes and his patient listening. Then his hands reached out and caressed mine, before his fingers walked along my arm, brushing and tickling my skin in a sign of what was to come.

"Are you hungry?" he asked.
"I could eat," I replied quickly.
"Well, let's get out of here then," he proposed.
"Let's go then."

I was ready, surprising myself with a bold move, a sense of clear direction, and a commitment to allow my desires to lead me for once in my life. I had not known I could be that free.

As we walked out, Ahmad grabbed me by the waist as we waited for his car. Then, as he lit a cigarette, I leaned close enough to breathe in his cologne. Mixed with the tobacco smoke, the scent took me back to the memory of the man I had summoned up in my midnight fantasies over the course of many moons.

Ahmad opened the car door for me, and we drove off. It wasn't long before he pulled onto a nearby residential street. There, at 1:00 am, as Wednesday became Thursday, the moon waited for the sun and couples floated away in shared dreams and individual fantasies. We were among them.

He had barely parked before he took his seat belt off. Without a word, he moved closer to me and began to kiss me as wildly as I had imagined. His kisses traveled up and down my neck, his lips and tongue covering every inch before landing on my mouth, connecting with my lips as if a magnet were pulling us together. Soon he moved his mouth over my chest, then onto my breasts, licking my nipples and looking up at me as I closed my eyes in ecstasy.

Once again, time was meaningless, place inconsequential. All I knew was that we were on the backseat, doing the wild dance from my dreams, being devoured and devouring, unapologetically.

To be wildly free. To feel my body alive in ecstasy.
To know with certainty that I am still alive.
That I feel intensely,
That I am beautiful beyond my flaws.

I can receive pleasure,
I can give it too.
But I was there to receive it.
All of it.

Ahmad's fingers inside of me made me levitate.
I traveled to the far east with him,
I sat with him
 And later,
 Walked the souks,
Learned Arabic,
Rode camels on the Sahara,
Came many times looking at Dubai
Right in his eyes,
Skydived over the fake sands
And became
Unaware that any of my fantasies
Really mattered
When
his kisses traveled
up and down
my body,
his sex in my mouth,
letting me ride his ancient world.

His pleasure made me tremble,
One more time,
On top of him.

We flew first class and landed,
bumping into the bright colors of a police car's flashing lights,
the stark, white beam of the policeman's flashlight
just outside our car's fogged windows.

We heard a knock on the glass.

"Please roll down the windows," the police officer said.
Ahmad quickly zipped his pants. I put on my blouse as he pressed the button that made the windows go down. The officer was already writing a ticket.
"You know this is indecent exposure, and I could arrest you? You do understand?"
"Yes, officer. We're very sorry. We'll be on our way home," Ahmad said.

The officer let us go and we laughed as we drove away, relieved we didn't have to end the night in prison after such a memorable experience. Ahmad suddenly stopped and said, "Are you still hungry?"
"I'm good," I answered, interpreting hunger in more than one way.

Ahmad drove me home and opened the passenger door. As I got out of his fancy car, he bent down and kissed me softly on my lips before saying, "I am flying to Abu Dhabi to stay with my parents next week. My student visa has expired. I hope we can keep in touch."
"Of course, Ahmad. I hope you have a wonderful trip back home."

I knew we would never speak again. We both knew. But it didn't matter. Both of us had already taken what we needed.
We humans believe that happiness consists of repetition,
Of once again reliving as many times as necessary what
awakens us.
Maybe it's the rarity of those magical instances that we are

here to surrender to...
However short or finite they may be.

I stood outside my home watching Ahmad drive away, realizing he was just a delicious gift from the universe to stimulate the creation of my new destiny. My joy was not about him: It came from a deeper place. I had tapped into my own inner world of passion and pleasure. I had opened the door to a life free of fears, where I could always step out and live my dreams.

Dancing my way into my bedroom, I suddenly felt the click — that moment when it all comes together, and everything makes so much sense. It didn't matter why I hadn't seen it before. I saw it now. This was the perfect time to do all those things I had put away for so long; all the hobbies and passions that I had abandoned. It was time to revive them all.

I began to keep a journal, beginning that night, and discovered forgotten longings, like my love for adventure and for Salsa dancing. I had studied dance as a child and, before getting married, I was often on the dance floors of Los Angeles. I had even taken classes with world champions. I remembered my first dance shoes, gold with silver accents, and the way I felt when I hit the dance floor. I spent hours there without any real sense of time. All I sensed was pure joy in the present moment. I was more and more alive with each movement. Laughter was the music that lightened every step. Sensuality and rhythm became one.

My soul started to speak. It was asking me to dance and explore again after so many years. I remembered a phrase my best friend Stephanie had once shared with me: *Querer es poder!* It means, if you want it badly enough, you can make it happen.

But my kids. But my budget. I couldn't have a babysitter come too often. I started to find reasons to put my dreams away.

Maybe I could ask my sister to stay at home with the kids so I could take my weekly dance classes again? I wondered. *Would that be selfish?*

Overly indulgent? Was I crazy for feeling this way?

I had to find out.

The next afternoon, I called my sister, Ari, and tested the waters.

It felt good to ask for help but it was something I had never been comfortable with. I was used to bearing everything alone. As a seasoned *giver*, it felt strange to put my needs first. But I loved my sister and my sister loved me, and I had barely said, "Could you…?"
Before she replied, "whatever you need."

The week flew by, and the night of my first dance class as a forty-year-old mother of three arrived. Dressing, I caught sight of my body in the mirror, and immediately judged it. I certainly did not look like I had back in the day. Why would I want to embarrass myself? How could I go out wearing a tight dress with these *lonjas*? Shame.

My body had been in retirement for too long, and it would be a good idea to leave it that way.

I started to cry. It was not easy to look at myself honestly and love my imperfections.

I grabbed the phone and called my sister so I could cancel and get back to my reality.
"Too late, Sis. Open the front door," she said down the line.

My beautiful sister stood on my porch and my inner critic was silenced by her smile.

"Okay girl, get ready… What are you going to wear?" she asked.
"I have not worn any of those dresses in such a long time."
"*Dale! Muéstrame*… Fashion show, fashion show…"
"No, seriously Sis, let's forget about it." A tiny tear rolled down my cheek. The inner critic was back.
"Are you crazy? Do you know how beautiful you are?"

My sister's hugs have always had powers over me, ever since we were kids. There was a sweetness to them that brought me back to some sort of paradise, where I felt unconditionally loved.

She seemed more excited than I did as she headed into my closet and took five dresses out.
"Try this one," she said.
"The red one?"
"Siiiiii!!!! Ese!!!!"

I looked at myself in the mirror and did a few basic dance steps. Then I moved back and forth across my bedroom, turning, shaking my hips and my shoulders as I flipped my long hair in my sister's face. We ended up on the floor laughing so hard that we started crying.

"I still got it, girl," I said.
"I guess you do," she replied, raising her beautiful thick brows. "This is the girl I always want to remember," she added, as we both got a little teary-eyed.

My sister helped me find my glittery purse before rolling up her sleeves and getting down on the floor to play video games with her nephews; my boys. I watched them for a few minutes before blowing them a kiss goodnight. I didn't think they would stop what they were doing, but they did.
"*Wow*, Mom you look *sooooo* beautiful!" the youngest said.
"Yeah — beautiful mom," the other two said, almost in unison.

I let those words sink in. I accepted them as a new kind of truth. A handsome stranger and a love for dancing had restored me to my most alive self, returning a version of my soul that had been buried for years. I vowed never to turn against myself again. Feeling this alive was something I would cherish forever.

I am alive.
I am beautiful.
I am free.

I hit the dance floor,
awakened to my soul's
awaited dance,
freestyle in my mind.

I jazz walk
All the way to the center of the stage,
My ice-cream hips
At last begin to taste sweet.

My arms soften
As they greet
my hair's
wild presence,

My mind gently telling me:

One more turn and
You will conquer your world.

What a gift it is
to feel
beautifully
free.

"I inspire tenderness in you, and you make me forget time,
death. I wonder if that is not what desire truly is:
Forgetting our own mortality."

A taste of Freedom

Dawn arrives amid Caribbean dancing, drums, heat, and pure desire. The sun remains hidden but sends rays of light to tease us. We can feel fate playing a role and we just can't let the night escape without knowing its game. Magical, colorful colonial homes line Colombia's cobblestone streets. We walk — or should I say 'float'? Arriving at *La Plaza de Santo Domingo* in Cartagena, we turn left, in search of a safe place.

We make love in a hostel, sharing the small room with weary travelers. They sleep in silence as we stifle the sounds of our burning passion, trying to remain strong. I surrender quickly. As you take me, I try to move away. But your pull melts my will. You want me to give you everything. As if it belongs to you. As if nothing is sacred.

You possess me with a passion that's almost savage. I close my eyes, but not to sleep. For the first time in my life, rest is meaningless. I am awake, alive, and drunk on the flames of love.

The moon gives way to the sun, to birds chirping, to my eyes opening and our bodies wrapped together. Your arms hold me in a grasp so tight I cannot pull away for even a second. Perhaps I am sleepwalking, as I watch you lying there asleep, naked, perfect, and wicked. Perhaps I am dreaming, as I return to your side and feel you cling to me. It's as if, in me, you have found someone you had once lost, someone you have been searching for. You cling to me and there is no escape.

The morning light wakes us in the old city. The fever of love stirs you and you rise. Once again you strip me bare and consume me. The wood creaks but we can't even whisper. Eight people sleep around us. Drunk on love, I still contain myself. You want to make love once, and then again, and again. I refuse, engaging in a war of wanting versus waiting.

Yes fighting *no*.

Can the body transmit something beyond sound, touch, or heat? Are we just riding a powerful wave of desire — cresting and crashing? Or is this a communion of souls pulled together by the pulse of recognition?

We speak the same language. We walk around the city, surrounded by an ancient fortress, reflecting on Shakespeare's existential fever and torrid love. You recite Hamlet to me in Spanish then ask me to repeat it in English: *To be or not to be...* For an instant, you are Hamlet and I am Ophelia. We make a game out of a new play. Madness slides down your throat like liquor and lingers on your lips. I observe you, hallucinating with your hidden truths.

I know nothing about you, don't understand you, can't define you. And yet you can lead me down this passionate path and I would follow you endlessly. But it's time to go.

>*A Summer Night's Dream,*
>*Where will it take us?*
>
>*Most importantly, where it will take me?*
>
>*I wish I could create something out of this love,*
>*a beautiful work of art I could preserve,*
>*but I can't create,*
>*I can't even concentrate.*
>
>*All I want is another day with you.*
>
>*Will I see you again?*
>*Will you call me?*
>*Will you see me?*
>*Travel to me — no matter the distance?*
>
>*Why am I already giving you so much power over my life?*
>*Why am I already drawn to you,*
>*Ready to go to you, wherever you are?*

Is it just to savor the energy of these passionate moments?
I would be lying if I said no.

But would I really go
anywhere you asked me to?
I would get lost in a sea of fantasies,
forget my meditation practice,
and jump on that boat of
intoxicating pleasure and
connection that I feel when
I am with you.

But I must center myself.

I must remember how dangerous this kind
of infatuation can be.
How weak it makes me feel
to be so easily controlled.

How can I say goodbye and forget about your passionate,
romantic soul?
Are you merely a reflection of what I seek to feel?
Have I created you?

The next day, I don't hear from you. I try to distract myself. I meet friends at the beach. But my mind keeps circling back to you.

I try to move on, but fail. It's not long before I'm thinking about you again, wondering where you are in this city of magic. I stop at a Cuban bar and lose myself in the rhythms of old salsa music and thirst-quenching mojitos. Then I walk along the beautiful streets of Getsemani. On every corner, street art and quaint new artisanal restaurants welcome me in a fusion with the city's ancient structures. I get lost in a dream of a different kind of life.

What would it be like to wake up to these beautiful sights and sounds every morning? Afro-Colombian music filling the air, and beautiful

Palenquera women parading through these historic streets paved with ancestral stories?

Since college, my life has been spent in another magical city: New York. But its skyscrapers and subways cast a different spell, one that comes at a very high price.

I have been living in shades of cement and concrete for too many years. Now, in Colombia, as I visit family, it all comes back to me. I can't help but feel vibrant and alive again. The colors, drained from my life, have returned.

What is stopping me from living in this new world that my soul now craves? I don't know. I don't have children. I have just finished my journalism degree. One could say I am free.

These are the thoughts that accompany me as I wander the streets in this beautiful old town where Gabriel Garcia Marquez's books seem to come alive. Where history tells a different story; one where the Spanish came and raided it all, using its natives as slaves. Today, those resilient spirits are still found walking — a little freer, yet enslaved nonetheless, by the chains of systematic racism.

The realities of the world are far more pressing than my privilege, yet here I am worrying about a summer love.

Could I ever do something to make a difference, or will I always be driven by egotistical longings? Could I write about what I have witnessed here and raise awareness of social issues?

I keep walking, pulling out my phone so I can point my camera at corner after corner. I capture images of colorful balconies filled with the brightest flowers. I walk to *La Ciudad Amurallada,* back to my hostel, and before going to the room I check at the front desk.

Has anyone has left a message for me?

Disappointed, I go upstairs and throw myself down on the lower bunk of my assigned wooden bed, knowing there's someone asleep above me. I pull the little curtain closed, hoping for some sense of privacy. I lay in bed, imagining a life filled with passionate kisses and Afro-Caribbean dance, and I fall asleep smiling.

I have no sense of time when suddenly my dreams are filled with his unmistakable scent and my hands are touching his body. Have I been asleep for minutes or hours? Am I asleep at all? There is someone in my space. I sense this is real, but I am not afraid. I know he has returned.

Jumping onto the balcony, climbing in the window on the second floor, he entered without being noticed. Guests are not allowed but he has found a way. He wants his way with me, as well. He makes that clear as he nestles alongside my body, pressing his body into me, becoming a part of my dream.

We made love all night, barely sleeping, straining to be as silent as possible. That was an exercise in futility: Only thin curtains separated us from the six hostel guests on the other bunk beds in the room. Needless to say, the colorful fabric did little to mute our sighs, bites, and muffled screams. There were endless orgasms and peals of laughter, made even louder by our funny-faced attempts to stifle them.

By 5am, we had fallen semi-asleep, but it didn't last long. By 8am, his embraces and a savage erection made us dance in bed again until a clear threat from the Australian traveler next to us got our attention. He was determined to turn us in to the hostel management.

I pulled the tiny curtain aside and, when the coast was clear, my 'guest' jumped back out of the window and onto the balcony leaving no trace of any such visitor. We agreed to meet around the corner by *La Tiendita del Reloj,* a little convenience store just below.

I danced out of bed and into the bathroom to freshen up — ten minutes was all I needed. My Caribbean tan made make-up completely unnecessary. My golden hair was tossed with happiness and wild sex. His love gave me a new kind of glow. A pair of white shorts, a loose white cotton top, and a pair of vintage aviator glasses did the job.

As I walked toward La Tiendita del Reloj, I was struck by the same feeling from the day before, the one I had when I was walking *in* Getsemani. I wanted to wake up every day with the beautiful sounds of the Caribbean. I wanted to say hello to humble but joyful people, who are always ready to greet the world with a warm *buenos días* and a smile.

I started to feel sad just thinking about going back to NYC. There, was a life I had grown accustomed to; it promised so much hope for 'success'. But somehow, somewhere along the way, I had lost my thirst for the kind of successful tomorrow that meant sacrificing the joys of today.

Sitting at a table across from one another, he drank a cold Club Colombia beer, and I got lost in his green eyes and his smile. It was as if I could see the future unfold.

He would leave soon, but this erotic adventure would remain. It had given me an opportunity to reignite a part of myself that had been dormant for a while. My passionate, spontaneous self had returned. I decided to stay in Cartagena for a few months. Now, I wanted a more meaningful life. And I wanted to be of service, to give back.

> *People used to tell me*
> *I had it all,*
> *But what they did not know*
> *Is that*
> *I silently wept*
> *Wondering*
> *Why I felt so empty,*
> *Looking for a way*
> *to be of service.*

Big cities,
Egos and responsibilities,
What can I do with my privilege?

If somehow,
I was this lucky,
If I could travel
And seek experiences,
That alone
Made me
Wonder,
What if everywhere
I went
I found a way to
Give and not only take?

This is where I am today,
Ready to embrace
A new way of living,

Where my heart
And my art
can truly make a difference.

"I crave to find that being that shreds me into poetry. Living poetry. Nothing shall ever replace the union of two beings governed by the same laws of desire and creation."

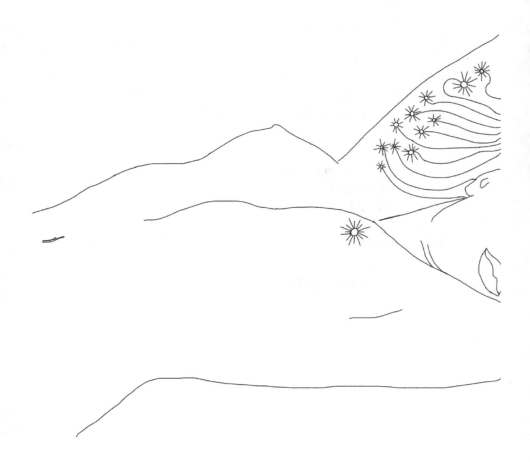

Mending My Heart

I know. Not all wives are sad. Once upon a time, I was a happy wife. It was during the most beautiful autumn I had ever witnessed: My autumn in Madrid. The crisp and ancient breeze of an unknown city gave me a renewed zest for living. That was when it started. He arrived. He entered my world, and before I knew what had happened, I was transformed. First, through love. Years later, through resentment.

Love stories are like that. There are winners and losers. Although I prefer to believe that in the end, everyone actually gets what they need. I prefer to think everyone is delivered to their destined place; the one fate has intended for them — before they were even born.

That autumn, we were perfect. In that exact place, at that exact moment in time, we both felt hopeless and yet we found our bodies gave us faith — our bodies came together as a quintessential dream and proof positive of our existence.

Yes, I was a happy wife during our travels through Spain. Holding hands, in our little bedroom in Madrid — our paradise of perfect passion, a humble yet sweet sanctuary, where we would eat chocolate bread in the nude. Wrapped only in sheets. Wrapped only in each other. Sometimes, we would play. I would drape myself with sheer frilly robes or body-hugging corsets. The light streaming in through the window warmed my skin and revealed the innocent glow of someone capable of loving in the present. The pain of the past vanished, and the future was worth waiting for. Why would we rush?

He drove me wild. He enveloped me with his love, and I could open up to him and be vulnerable. Dancing in the name of love, I loved him mercilessly as he landed beside me, inside me, over me. Before the war, his work, the clouds — before the skies took him away.

I, the happy lover, became the waiting lover. Every minute he was away was a minute I would save, storing my energy for him. Awaiting his return. Feeling the thrill of his breath and his body arriving even before I opened the door for him. The joy of seeing him standing there, wearing his perfectly ironed military uniform, stepping into our home. At that precise moment, he seemed more beautiful to me than ever. Perfectly beautiful.

Undressing quickly, I would surprise him by revealing a black or red corset underneath my clothes. Then I would spend all morning making myself look like a muse, like his fantasy. How I wanted to become his goddess, his Venus, his everything. It wasn't long before these exact erotic rituals rendered me lifeless. I went from muse, to abused, to prey.

He was deployed to Houston, Texas. That's when our lovers' games grew darker.

The stress of a new life, of new beginnings, challenged our idyllic love. Our flame extinguished, we settled for dull, domestic love.

Playful, fiery intimacy took a turn. If it was there at all, it was unrecognizable. Once filled with magic, our love was empty. No longer driven by desire, there was only desperation, expectation, and duty. That's when the unhappy wife appeared.

The eager lover became the exhausted wife, forced to keep up a daily sex schedule, all while performing chores. Dances of love began to smell of everyday olive oil and chicken. The scent of *Jean Paul Gaultier* perfume on my body began to fade away.

His PTSD erupted, releasing a buried anger from his traumatic childhood in Nicaragua. He had seen loved ones murdered in the name of *La Revolución*. After many years of witnessing these horrific crimes, he was consumed.

And I was the one who held him close as he remembered. I was the one bearing witness to it all. Eventually, I was the only one who could fill his void, by becoming a living war zone.

Psychotic episodes, fueled by his already possessive nature, drove him to madness.

"Where do you think you are going dressed like that?" he would ask me.
"I am going to work, and then to my radio internship," I replied.
In his eyes, I was always dressed too sexy.
"Open your coat, let me see what you are wearing," he would insist, before undressing me with his glare.

Locked inside our bedroom.
Being recorded 24/7.
Phone lines tapped.
Our new reality.

Gone were the nights of the smiling military man behind the door, when the sounds of war were eclipsed by our moans of love. When the weight of his weapon was extinguished in the softness of my hands. When he held me with passion and sweetness, with a grasp so gentle and unusual for someone so strong.

I began to miss small things — the presents he brought from some base or port. Simple trinkets that, although lacking in luxury, carried the aroma of his thoughts. With me, he had become a child, hugging me in the nude and learning to walk, talk, dream, to be himself. Before the pain drove him away.

With me, he came to understand there was another world, one with a God, and free of the explosions that ripped through legs, heads, and arms; free of mutilated and dying bodies. In me, he found his piece of heaven and in him, I thought I had found love.

Once the unhappy wife appeared, she lingered. Over time, a daily sameness made us forget that our love was a miracle, that life had given hope back to us. We forgot how to laugh, once everyday concerns replaced delicious kisses with strained bank accounts, when going out felt like working overtime. Everything started to crumble around us. In us. The damn daily war to survive sent us into battle, turned us both into soldiers on a mission of lesser value, one that left us naked and alone, deprived of the life from our love.

The drudgery of soulless work, obsessing over finances — the 'day-to-day' — replaced our spontaneity, our magical ways of loving each other. Compliments became criticism, and then even the sad wife retreated, and replaced her once-upon-a-time lover with loneliness. We were left all alone, my loneliness and I — left to remember happier days, when it was just the two of us walking through *El Retiro*, daydreaming in Madrid, living the purest of moments, the kind that are lived when one is truly in love and is loved back with the same fierce flame.

War wounded him and took him away from me. Sadness fooled me and took me to an imaginary world, where there was also no love to be found. Loneliness kept me looking for love anywhere and everywhere except within.

His mental disease got the better of him. He began to control me. If he wasn't following me, he was having me followed by others. Everyone around me told me I had to escape before it was too late. I got a restraining order. It made him so angry he threatened to kill me. That was before he was taken away. One of his soldiers stepped in, and he was committed to a military psychiatric facility.

Heartbreak.

*

It has been almost a year since we ripped ourselves apart and went our separate ways. Somehow each minute still etches a longing for him. If not for tangible evidence, if not for those who remind me of the pain, the meanness, the shadows, if not for all that and more, I would forget the wives that weren't happy. Or worse: I would blame myself for how things came to an end. But, somewhere inside of me, there is a woman who knows better.

Could I tolerate the pain of war? The military tone of his voice? The controlling air of the demanding soldier who issues orders? It is with shame that I say, *yes*, I would trade this solitude for his touch, his green eyes seeing into my soul, I would trade this silence for his voice saying he loves me in a tone befitting a general. It was a tone that I knew was not the most romantic, but that I will always believe was sincere.

Yes, time has the dual ability to become a spell and a compass, a remembrance and a massacre of memories. Losing my way, I knew there was something more to find. Still, this loss was so permanent. When will I finally be free?

If I was given the chance to rewrite our story, how would I finish it? We would have been lovers forever, living in Madrid and forgetting the cruelty of the world.

Where will I go now?

Where will I begin?

I have no idea,

But one thing is certain:

I have to start from zero.

Create a new life.

Seek support.

Get close to family.

Mend my heart.

Pick-up the broken pieces.

Come to terms with my role in it.

Heal my trauma.

Seek the company of other women.

Believe in divine guidance.

Honor every step of my grieving process.

Embrace change.

Forgive myself.

And most importantly,

Love myself.

"The lover must win many battles, but the
main one will be against herself."

"I was not born to lead a normal life,
nor to have normal loves."

Buena Vista Motel

At thirty-two years of age, she had never visited a motel. She had seen them in movies, in torrid love scenes, but something about them went against her morals. She thought they were in poor taste for virtuous women. But that afternoon, love surprised her. It was another busy afternoon at work, another Friday packed with meetings and trouble at the TV network.

Their sexual chemistry began very soon after meeting on the job. She was a young journalist, and he was a seasoned radio personality. Soon, they discovered they had one thing in common: They both loved falling in love with love — or what they mistakenly interpreted as love, living in that heavenly space somewhere between passion and infatuation.

Passion was their language.

Flirting across sterile hallways
And conference rooms,

Working hard during the weekdays
To celebrate on their special days.

Secret meetings
That became their weekly
Meetings
With dangerous
And delicious
Passion.

Fridays, after work, were the only days for love and fire. After a hard week, it was common for a group of co-workers to head for a bar and let loose. So they waited for Friday, every week, to give them the excuse they could use at home. Laying out their lies, little lies, white lies, they could feel lust that went beyond sin. Tangled between their lips was the complicity of love.

Once they were together, on those Fridays, they could say everything they needed to with a kiss and the first drink of the evening. Truth and relief were followed by laughter and gossip about everyone at the station.

At five o'clock, they brushed knees on tall bar stools. By six o'clock, they had made their way to reclining leather seats in his car. A kiss, fervent and long, would lead them to the madness of believing they loved each other. Their lips traveled down necks, chests, breasts, landing on the sweetest spots, their most intimate of places, clearing a path to the inevitable. Occasionally, he would remember to look out for possible passers-by who might discover and even identify them. Soon, desire was unstoppable: tongues, arms, genitals, gazes, all while the smoke from their breath clouded the glass.

On this particular Friday, after he cracked open the window and lit a cigarette, after the smoke swirled around itself, he started the car and followed a route she didn't recognize. They drove down neighboring streets, down lonely streets, down dark streets, down inaccessible streets, down roads being repaired, past corners without witnesses, until they reached the Buena Vista Motel. In spite of its gray appearance, it seemed to welcome love. With two glasses of wine soothing her, she could laugh at her inner voice. She no longer heard the warnings from the nuns at school. She could ignore the rules for 'good girls', laid out by her wealthy family in Peru.

Now the beautiful lovers went up the stairs that were as dull as the grey sky. They entered this place of ancient white, beige touchups, and forgotten wrought iron. The bed, with its silver-tinged bedspread, didn't bother her either. She dared to sit on it, watching her lover close the door, turn, and approach. Throwing himself on the bed, they started rolling and laughing, her pearl necklace flipping and twisting. As she removed it, the voice she heard was her own, saying, *'I can't believe I'm here.'* She said it with embarrassment and excitement, and she knew she would remember this moment every day of her life. She had gone through long periods without experiencing what she called: *the fire of feeling.* Now, with him, she was alive again.

He was an alpha male, a seasoned radio executive but a poet on the inside, worldly and street-smart, multilingual. The kind of man who finds power in his position and his impact on the world. But he was noble, with a youthful demeanor and refined taste, and all that won her over — his choice of the finest cognac when dining, his obsession with the neatness and cleanliness of his car. All of these details were, in her view, the marks of status and class she was searching for in a man. She knew that only a man with these qualities would resemble her father and the elegance she loved about him.

Every Friday was an invitation to believe they loved one another. As the months went by, the love built to such a degree that jealousy stepped in, as their vows of 'hearts possessed' made them believe they had a right to ownership.

That was what she felt when, one evening, after an Italian dinner, his wife called him. He interrupted the magic of their moment by leaving the table, but she could still hear him say *'I love you'* to his dear wife when the call was over. Those words devastated her. Under the influence of liquor, they echoed even louder, as if they negated the entire reality of their days together. She was, and would always be, only the lover, the woman with whom he would live a passing yet profound ecstasy, where he could be young again. It was only with her that he could share his domestic frustrations and find release.

On the best nights, this release came in the form of seven orgasms, something only she could provide, making him feel virile and manly again. He had spent years in a fireless relationship and only she allowed him to revive his worth.

Seven times; seven deaths and seven resurrections; seven times when she was petrified of the possibility of killing him during a night of love and being responsible for such a crime. But she soon learned that those orgasmic deaths of her lover were the reason why he felt alive again, and ready to take on new challenges in his life. The more alive he felt, the more he depended upon her to play her role in his life, and the more she needed to be with him — it was more than a need, it was an infatuation.

This sense of entitlement started to make her an unhappy lover. Soon, she began to love him in the worst way possible, mixing love and desire together. It was an uncontrollable force — and it gave him more power over her than he deserved.

She began to feel jealous of his wife, to feel empty when he left motel rooms while she stayed behind, lying as if in a light levitation. It was the perfect mood for composing songs, or playing the guitar, but disastrous too. It encouraged a melancholy that ended up suffocating her, and making her feel weak. And she began to wonder if these passionate encounters had just become *commonplace* for him, while she was still defining them as *special*.

How could she transform this newfound aliveness
Without feeling depleted?

How could pleasure invigorate her
Instead of diminishing her?

Would she decide not to see him again,
Or just see him on her own terms?

She did not know how it would play out just yet,
But one thing was certain:

She would take responsibility for her actions.
She would discover, in due time,
What awaited her on the other side.

Pleasure, just as pain,
has a price, she thought.

"Paradise contains her passion and fire.
Her nudity is a perfect garden."

Shakti

Amara woke, got up and put on her healing music, which included a dose of Lila Downs and Chavela Vargas. Then she took a warm bath, soaking in her own mix of earthy essential oils, and cleansed away her bad dreams.

On a typical day, there was nothing in the world that brought her as much joy as walking through those ancient cobblestone streets in Coyoacán. Mornings, however, were especially sacred. They brought a sense of continuity and fluidity to her life — greeting all the shop owners around her home, drinking her black coffee, always with a cigarillo — she loved it all. But that morning, from the moment she opened her eyes, something did not feel right. The night had been filled with the terror of that recurring, unwelcome nightmare that had visited her for years.

Over time, Amara had been cultivating the tradition of opening a book to a random page every morning, in order to find a special message for her day ahead. It was a superstitious habit that made her feel like there was indeed a higher being, always sending her messages in subtle ways.

On that summer morning, she decided to reach for a seventy-year-old, first edition poetry collection by Sor Juana Inés de La Cruz. Opening the well-thumbed volume, the pages flipped, and her fingers randomly landed on page 85. It was a right-hand page, and the words streaming down it read:

"Finjamos que soy feliz,
triste pensamiento, un rato;
quizá podréis persuadirme,
aunque yo sé lo contrario..."
— Sor Juana Inés de la Cruz

(Let's pretend that I am happy,

sad contemplation, for a while;
perhaps you could persuade me,
but I know it's a lie...)

Was she happy? Most of the time. At least that's what Amara told herself, although she knew otherwise. She couldn't deny that her self-imposed celibacy had become unhealthy. Perhaps the poem was a sign, she thought. Perhaps it was telling her to embrace her sexuality once again, opening herself to more pleasure and happiness.

So, after her bath, she let her towel drop to the floor and chose to dress in the color of the sun. In spite of feeling a little sadder than usual, she began her morning ritual by inviting everything light and beautiful to join her as she walked through Coyoacán. She felt the cobblestones under her feet as she made her way to her favorite bakery, where she knew she would be surrounded by books and the awakening sounds of La Plaza.

Mexico City was the perfect backdrop to her existence. She wanted to live there until her death, when she would have her ashes scattered over Xochimilco by friends and family as they listened to *bolero* music.

She had no desire to travel, even if she had the funds for it. In this city she had it all, everything she ever wanted was just a short walk away. It was a city filled with such contrasts and culture and so much life that she never yearned to be anywhere else.

As for her recurring bad dreams? They were always a variation on the same theme. They always included a man who kept hiding from her; a man who she desperately wanted to make love to. He disappears at every corner until they finally meet and make love. However, when they do, she can't bring herself to have an orgasm.

She had sought out all kinds of therapy, traditional and non-traditional, even considering the healing benefits of *ayahuasca*.

Fifty years of life, and still, when she least expected, those nightmares would wake her. Tears flowed as her whole body trembled and she shook in her bed, divorced and alone.

She had been married once, briefly, which was time enough to realize it was not for her, despite social obligations. She ignored the constant gossip from people she did not care about:

"Amara will end up spending her days alone, pobrecita. *Without even any children! Who will take care of her?"*

She had heard it all.

Every time she heard this kind of commentary on her way of life, she would smile compassionately — but also sarcastically. She was certain that all those gossipers, who were so harsh and insensitive about her life choices, were frustrated housewives or cheating spouses who only wished they could enjoy a taste of her freedom. Clearly, they never had that chance.

She had known many women throughout her life who, unable to get an education, were dependent upon the income of a partner. They had to submit themselves to someone else's rule.

Pragmatic by nature, and spiritually a mother without ever conceiving a child, Amara had always dreamed of creating an all-female commune. There, women who lacked the means to afford their own housing could get away from abusive partners — they would come and live in this haven of peace, a retreat, an oasis where their pain could be washed away, where they could finally listen to their own minds and bodies. She recognized that without a safe space, women were restricted from living fully — limits were placed on their dreams, and finding pleasure on their own terms was next to impossible.

The more she thought about that dream, the more she thought about how much she had… and nothing made sense. She had a safe space. She enjoyed financial and emotional freedom. She didn't depend upon anyone but herself. Yet she was still blocked when it came to experiencing pleasure. Why?

It was time to seek the help of a *curandera* friend who had mentioned a Yoni class, where women learned to self-pleasure in sacred ways that proved transcendental for many.

Where does one's pleasure hide
When it decides to bury its rays?

Do we become so numb that we forget
There is a vortex of sunlight
Dormant inside of us?

Awaken, divine Goddess,
Within you there is a world
Which connects heaven and earth.

Awaken, Muse of Muses,
From the sleep of lies
That have told you
You are here to sacrifice.

Pleasure and joy
Are your birthright.

Before heading to La Curandera's home, Amara grabbed a book she had once bought at a quaint used bookstore. It was about Hinduism and contained a word that had sparked her curiosity — *Shakti*.
Female Power.
The Feminine force from which everything is created and destroyed.

La Curandera's home was more like a botanical garden filled with all kinds of plants, herbs and cacti. On a little white door in the center of it all, a sign read:

'Acá vive la luz de tu deseo.'
(Here the light of your desire lives.)

Desire?
Amara took in the word as if she had forgotten what desire was — because she had.

La Curandera greeted her with holy hands, wrinkled and freckled from the sun, and a naughty smile. Then, together, they walked through a narrow corridor into the main garden where, much to Amara's surprise, small statues of Hindu goddesses appeared — the same goddesses that had caught her attention in the book. They were accompanied by clay figurines of *Coatlicue*, the Aztec goddess recognized for her power when it came to fertility, life, death and rebirth.

La Curandera pointed to the straw floor and asked Amara to lay down within a circle of red and white candles. Then, she was asked to close her eyes so La Curandera could take her on a healing journey, one she practiced on women whose connection to feminine power had been lost.

Her voice was hypnotic as her words flowed out, as if Amara was listening to poetry or birdsong.

> "Mira, *you can never forget that you are the greatest creature in this universe.*
> *Within you, the power of a million matriarchs is imprinted along with the key to unlocking life's secrets. It is the key to true union and love, not only with others but, most importantly with yourself.*
>
> "Allow yourself to feel pleasure as much as, or more than, you allow yourself to cry.
> *Pleasure is also a cleansing energy.*
> *You just have to choose wisely who you share your energy with,*
> *Not everyone is deserving of your divine energy, the energy of Shakti.*
>
> "You see, you are both a goddess and a warrior,
> *A mother and a lover,*
> *And you must learn to live the duality of your nature.*
> *If you lose your balance,*
> *You begin to lose your power.*
>
> "There is another thing.

Don't let others take your power from you.
You see, there are people that want to rob you
Of your time and energy.
They just want to deplete you.
That's the greatest danger.

"You must defend your sacred time on this earth
From anyone, no matter how close they are to you,
Even family members,
Who want to take from you what they lack in themselves.
I tell you,
Defiende, pelea,
Defend, fight if necessary
To maintain your sacred energy and protect your time.

"The Diosa *and* Guerrera *energy that lives within you,*
Is yours alone
and only you should decide how and with whom it is shared.
Remember not to let anyone give you more pleasure than you
can give yourself.

"Toma,
Take this.
I am going to introduce you to the knowledge of sacred
pleasure."

She handed Amara a smooth piece of rose quartz in the shape of an egg, then lit some *copal* and played indigenous music, filling the room with the sounds of flutes and running water. Then, she asked Amara to open her legs and brush the cool egg along her thigh before slipping it inside her vagina.

"Relájate, estás muy tensa.
You are too stiff,
Relax!
The coldness of the crystal will soon be consumed by your fire.
Now slowly start moving your hips,

Rocking back and forth,
Feel the awakening,
That is taking place, and
Breathe deeply.

"Inhale through your nose
And exhale through your mouth,
Don't be embarrassed to make sounds,
Any sounds,
They are music from the depths of the earth.

"You see, we women have been taught to be quiet,
Because men have always known that our voices
Are so powerful.
That is why they have tried to muffle us
For centuries.

"There you go. That's right.
Relax a little more
And let the sweetness of your own being
Fill you with the best honey,
The best potion for seduction.
Feel how you begin to flow
Like water, moist and free,
Ever flowing.

"Now, start touching your own body,
Acknowledging the beauty that lies
Between your thighs and belly,
The secrets that are being released
From your waist and breasts.

"Women;
We are a field of gold and flowers.

"Now, touch your own lips,
Savor them with your tongue,

And discover the nectar you have
been keeping locked inside.

"This is your nectar,
Which only the privileged will taste
If you decide to gift it to them.

"Continue breathing,
As you remember that
This Shakti energy is always available to you
At any time,
And no one can take this away from you.

"Now, caress your breasts.
These are the most powerful slopes
Of your body's landscape,
They hold the kingdom of pleasure between them,
And they hold the power of both the mother and the goddess.
Treat them like the most valued gateway to your inner empire.

"Now, let your hands slide to your belly,
The eternal cave of birth and rebirth,
Where all mysteries of the universe lie.
Here is where your intuition will begin to warn you
When something or someone has evil intentions.
Listen carefully.

"Breathe deeply,
Remember to let all sounds become your own
Symphony.
They are yours to own and treasure.

"Finally, let your fingers come to your Yoni,
The temple of creation,
The royal seat of a goddess' power.

"Your Yoni has the power to start wars and end

Revolutions,
Its powers can be used both for evil and good,
So make sure you act accordingly.

"Here is where your final destination to the world of pleasure
Begins and ends, here is where both your art and your power
Will find inspiration.

"Let yourself be carried away by stardust and
Poetry, this is your own portal to liberation."

Amara gasped for air. Her skin felt a sudden wave of supercharged electricity and she finally let out a huge sigh of relief. The waves of ecstasy traveled through each inch of her body, awakening it from a profound dream of lethargy and loss. Then, tears began to pour uncontrollably, as if she had not cried in years. And finally, a deep sense of lightness imbued her whole being.

La Curandera came in again and brought a special *remedio*, a warm infusion with cacao and cinnamon, before sending Amara on her way.

"This remedio is a reminder of the warmth and fire that must never die within you, to maintain your well-being and help you accomplish your divine mission on this earth."

Amara walked away from La Curandera's home with a feeling she had not experienced since her youth. She headed home, choosing La Marquesa, a different street than she usually traveled. Here, she found everything as new and vibrant as when she had first moved to Mexico City, ten years before.

Amara walked home, opened the windows, and took a warm bath before going to bed. That night, she slept like a baby for the first time in over a decade — and on that summer night, the recurring dreams stopped, and on every night that followed, the nightmares never visited her again.

10 Commandments
for Happy Women

I will love myself above all, even when I feel unlovable.

I won't worship a partner to the point where she or he feels like the owner of my life.

I will never waste my tears in vain.

I will celebrate myself throughout all stages of my life.

I will honor my ancestors, especially the women that came before me.

I won't let my soul wither away, living a life that kills my truest essence.

I will never make love to anyone without feeling it. My body is my temple. I am the only who can decide when I want to share it.

I won't let anyone steal my joy, my dreams, or my ideals.

I will speak my truth, even if it makes others feel uncomfortable.

I won't envy other women, but will become their ally, as together we build a new vision for all women around the world.

Davina Ferreira is an award-winning entrepreneur, poet & founder of Alegría Media & Publishing, an indie publishing company @alegriamagazine that connects the world with Latinx books & magazines.

Ferreira was born in Miami but grew up in Colombia. She is the quintessential symbol of the immigrant's American Dream. Upon arriving in the U.S. Ferreira attended college, receiving a B.A. in Fine Arts from UC Irvine and worked as an actress at with the Bilingual Foundation of the Arts. Later on, she attended The Royal Academy of Dramatic Art in London (RADA) to pursue classical acting.

Ferreira then completed a Journalism Certificate at UCLA Extension and began a career in journalism, which led her to launch ALEGRÍA Magazine. She then wrote her first book, *Take Me with You/Llévame Contigo,* a bilingual compilation of short stories and poems of love. Her second book, *Finding My ALEGRIA* is an inspirational self- help memoir, which she hopes will motivate young entrepreneurs around the world to pursue their dreams regardless of their circumstances.

Ferreira has received The Rising Star Award by the prestigious National Latina Business Women Association, and the Latina of Influence Award by Hispanic Lifestyle magazine. Also, she received the CSQ Magazine New Gen Award for entrepreneurs at the Rockefeller Center in New York City.

During 2020, Oprah Magazine recognized her for bringing bilingual books to the LatinX community via her ALEGRIA Mobile Bookstore.

She is a sought-after speaker; whose passion is to inspire others to succeed as creative entrepreneurs. Some of her most memorable experiences include speaking at Harvard's Latina Lead Conference & Google's Women's summit.

In her free time, Ferreira volunteers bringing her ALEGRIA Mobile Bookstore to at risk youth in Los Angeles Country and she teaches creative writing & wellness workshops for women.

Her new poetry collection, *If love Had a Name* debuted last year.
This year, she is launching a new short story collection titled:
Stories of Happy Lovers & Unhappy Wives.

Write your own erotic poetry/stories

_____

_____

_____

_____

_____

_____

_____

_____

_____

_____

_____

_____

_____

_____

_____

_____

_____

_____

_____

_____

_____